"The Little Leftovers Have A Magical Christmas!"

is Dedicated to my Wonderful Pre-K,

Kindergarten, First, Fifth-and-Sixth Grade Students,

both past and present,

who have always Given me so much Joy

and sincerely Touch my Life in so many ways!

They will remain Forever in my Heart!

Starky Star was a striking sight
on a shelf in Dilly's Department Store.

He was so excited, yet full of suspense.
After all, today was Christmas Eve!
Starky knew this was his last chance
to spend Christmas with a very
special family.

Starky tried to smile at all the people as they passed by. But they didn't seem to notice. Everyone was in such a big hurry. "Last minute shoppers trying to do everything in one day!" Mr. Sell, the store manager, would always remark.

Starky was really beginning to get worried. It would soon be closing time. He felt a little better though, when he saw Tingles Tinsel, Garnie Garland and Lila Lights in their spots too.

All of a sudden, the store lights began to dim. He could hear the gentle voice of Mr. Sell saying, "The store will close in five minutes. Merry Christmas Everyone!"

Mr. Sell tried to reassure the Little Leftovers. "Cheer up! Surely, someone will take you home the day after Christmas when we have our Super Sale. I'm sure you have been left here for a very special reason," he said in a soothing voice.

Just then, the lights dimmed and the Little Leftovers heard the key turn in the lock.

That was it! They would be spending Christmas all alone on the same old shelves.

Tingles was teary-eyed, Garnie grieved
and Lila looked lost. Starky sniffed back tears.
What a sad sight they made indeed!

Suddenly, a big gust of wind blew the door wide open! "What was that?" Lila whispered in a soft voice.

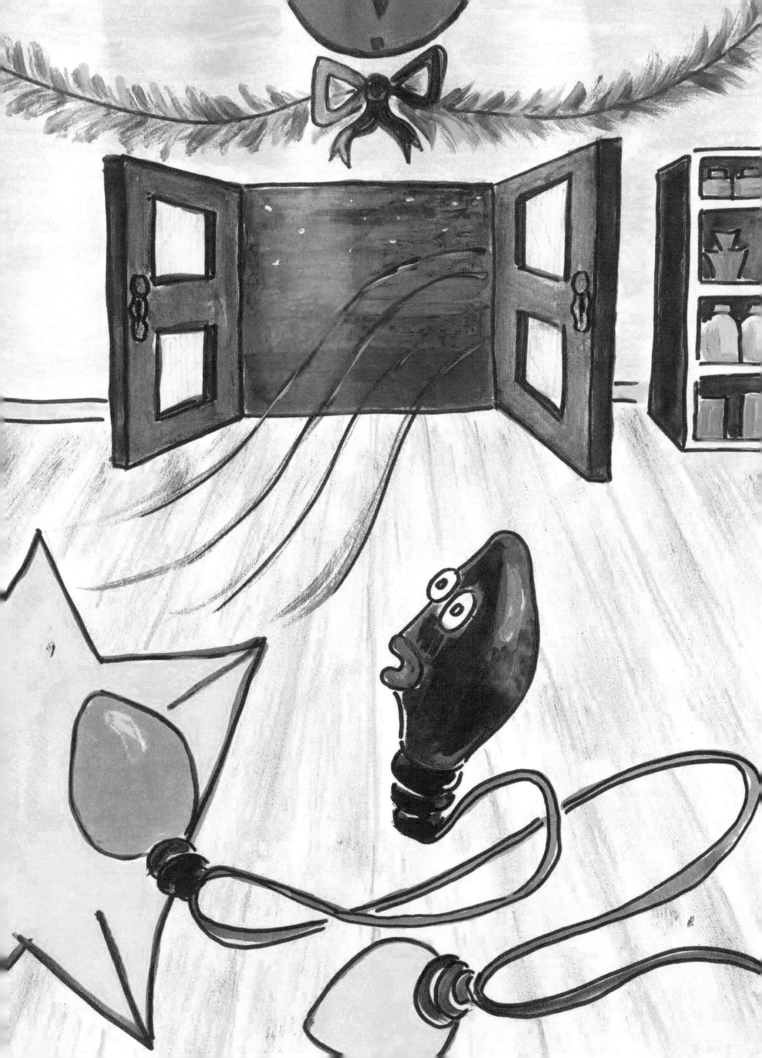

But the Little Leftovers could only stare straight ahead in shock and surprise. For standing right in front of them dressed in a red suit, was a stout man with a white beard and a big round belly!

"Ho! Ho! Ho!" said the man with a grin. Starky could scarcely believe what he was seeing. It was Santa Claus!

"Come with me!" Santa Claus said in a loud booming voice. "I have a special surprise for each of you!"

The Little Leftovers quickly slid off the shelves and slipped into Santa's cloth sack. "Ho! Ho! Ho!" he called out again.

Santa Claus led them to a ridged roof where his reindeer awaited.

He placed Starky, Tingles, Garnie and Lila on his sleigh and off they went!

They passed over many small villages
and towns, flying over rooftops of all
different shapes and sizes.

Snow began to fall gently as they hurried along. Glancing down, Starky was amazed at the beautiful scene below as everything seemed to snuggle up under a cozy white blanket of new fallen snow.

Over and over again, the big sled paused on colorful rooftops. On each one, Santa grabbed toys from his sack and delivered them to the children anxiously waiting below!

Finally, Santa rechecked his list one more time.

"All done," he said happily! "It's time to head home!"

"Where was home?" the Little Leftovers wondered.

Just then they heard, "Last stop! Everybody off! We're home!"

Wow! The Little Leftovers couldn't believe it – They were at the North Pole! Everything imaginable was emblazed in lights of all different sizes and colors which lit up the night like a giant fireworks display.

Santa Claus gently carried the Little Leftovers into the huge house.

As they looked around the large, cheerful room, they saw colorful stockings hanging over a big, crackling fireplace.

They were greeted pleasantly by Mrs. Claus, who was swinging back and forth in her freshly painted rocking chair. She was knitting a scarf, a last minute gift for Santa.

The Little Leftovers turned to see lots of little elves coming into the room carrying broken-down toys in their frail arms.

Mrs. Claus explained how each year they honored all the retired elves and old discarded toys who had given many years of service to children all around the world.

Everyone's attention was then drawn to the far right corner of the room where a big Christmas Tree stood, looking droopy, lonely and forlorn.

She was truly the prettiest color green Starky had ever seen!

"Cheer up, Chrissy! I brought you some new friends," Santa said. He explained that Chrissy had been very sad, so he had hoped the Little Leftovers could make her feel better. "Can you help Chrissy come to life?" he asked them.

"We can sure try!" Tingles said enthusiastically. So one by one, Tingles, Lila and Garnie gingerly stepped up to find cozy spots on Chrissy's outstretched branches.

At last, it was Starky's turn! Very cautiously, he began to crawl to the top, making sure not to step on any of his friends who were already adorning Chrissy's beautiful branches. It was a long climb, but finally, he made it to the top! Carefully, Starky positioned himself at the highest tip of the tree!

As Starky settled in snuggly, Chrissy suddenly came to life! She was beaming with joy! Soon everyone began to sparkle and twinkle with delight! Starky was thrilled to see his friends so happy!

Everyone in the room began to clap and cheer! Starky felt all squishy inside. As he glanced around, Starky knew this was going to be the best Christmas they ever had!

Yes, the Little Leftovers now had a family to love and cherish! And that made them all very happy indeed!

Author

Maryann McMahon is a Passionate, Lifelong Educator and Enthusiastic Children's Book Author. She has worked for many years as an Early Childhood and Elementary School Teacher, Assistant Principal and Pre-K Director. This is her 4th Published Book.

Illustrator

Agata Olszewska is an Avid Art Instructor of Early Childhood and Elementary School Children, as well as an Accomplished Illustrator. She has Collaborated on 3 Books with Maryann McMahon.

ISBN: 978-1-7320725-4-1

Made in the USA
Middletown, DE
14 November 2020